Just Call Me Joe

Just Call Me Joe

Frieda Wishinsky

Orca Book Publishers

National Library of Canada Cataloguing in Publication Data
Wishinsky, Frieda

Just call me Joe / Frieda Wishinsky.

"An Orca young reader"

ISBN 1-55143-249-8

I. Title.

PS8595.I834J87 2003 jC813'.54 C2003-910400-1

PZ7.W78032J87 2003

Library of Congress Catalog Card Number: 2003107504
Summary: Life in New York City in the early twentieth century is tougher than Joseph ever dreamed it would be.

Teachers' guide available at www.orcabook.com

Orca Book Publishers gratefully acknowledges the support of its publishing programs provided by the following agencies: the Department of Canadian Heritage, the Canada Council for the Arts, and the British Columbia Arts Council.

Cover design by Christine Toller
Cover illustration by Don Kilby
Interior illustrations by Stephen McCallum
Printed and bound in Canada

Orca Book Publishers is proud to demonstrate its commitment to the responsible use of our natural resources. This book is printed on Bioprint Paper supplied by Transcontinental Printing. Bioprint paper is 100% recycled, 100% post-consumer waste, processed chlorine-free, 100% Ancient-Forest free, and acid-free, using soy based inks.

IN CANADA
Orca Book Publishers
1030 North Park Street
Victoria, BC Canada
V8T 1C6

IN THE UNITED STATES
Orca Book Publishers
PO Box 468
Custer, WA USA
98240-0468

05 04 03 • 5 4 3 2 1

For my friends Kathy Kacer and Penny Fransblow and with thanks to Esther Sarah Evans.

Chapter One

Sometimes They Send You Back

"We're here! We're in America!" shouted Joseph, waving his cap in the air.

All around him people shouted and waved, as the ship passed the gleaming lady with the torch, the Statue of Liberty. It was as if all the misery of the last three weeks, the smells and sickness of too many people packed too tightly together, had disappeared into the early morning fog.

"Joseph! Your cap ... " said his 17-year-old sister, Anna. But before she could finish her sentence, Joseph's brown cap flew out of his hand.

Oh no! thought Joseph as he watched his cap ride the waves like a toy boat and then sink into the Atlantic.

"Oh, Joseph," said Anna. "Papa made it for you."

Joseph sighed. It was true. Papa had made it for him, but he couldn't let losing a cap spoil this wonderful day.

"It was already old and torn, Anna," said Joseph. "In America, I will buy a new cap. In America, I will buy an American cap."

Anna said nothing, but Joseph knew what she was thinking. He was thinking it too.

Mama. Papa.

At that moment, he would have given all the gold in America to have Mama and Papa there beside them.

Joseph closed his eyes and imagined his parents as they looked the last time he saw them. Papa, tall and stooped from days hunched over his sewing machine, tears flowing down his cheeks as he kissed his children goodbye. And Mama, her curly hair tinged with gray, whispering over and over, "Take care of each other."

But Joseph didn't want to think about his parents now. It hurt too much. It was better to remember how good it would be never to be frightened again by murderous Russian soldiers sneaking up on you in the woods or bursting into your house at night. Three months ago a drunken soldier had found him gathering mushrooms in the woods and pointed a gun at his head. "Next time you won't be so lucky, Jew," he'd warned. And a week later, two of Joseph's 14-year-old cousins had not been so lucky. They were murdered in the neighboring shtetl, a small town much like Joseph's own.

Night after night, for a week after their deaths, Papa and Mama stayed up late talking. Then, early Sunday morning, they told Anna and Joseph they had made a decision.

"You must go to America," said Papa. "We have just enough money for your passage. Anna, you are old enough to find work and look after Joseph. My sister Sophie in New York will help you. She is on her own since her husband died two years ago and she has no children. We will come as soon as we can."

Papa had placed his warm hand on Joseph's shoulder. "And you will help Anna, Joseph. You are strong and smart."

Papa was right.

So what if he was only ten? So what if he was short for his age and skinny as a stick? Didn't he outwit that bully Mendel? Mendel was taller and stronger than Joseph, but that didn't matter. Joseph had tied Mendel's laces to the table at heder, their school, last week, and Mendel had crashed to the floor before he could snatch Joseph's bread.

"I'll get you for this," Mendel sneered.

"Me?" said Joseph, in an innocent voice. "I'm not good at knots."

A tug at his sleeve woke Joseph from his thoughts. "Look Joseph," said Anna. "Look at New York City. It's so big."

Joseph's eyes widened as he looked up at the skyline. Buildings like castles towered side by side. It was all so tall, so new, so unknown. So different from the shtetl with its low wooden buildings all jumbled together. He knew every house, every farm, every tree in the shtetl. He knew every wagon and stand in the bustling marketplace where the peasants sold their fish, grain and vegetables and where he helped Mama sell the pants and shirts Papa sewed.

In America he knew nothing. Nothing now, but soon he'd be walking down a real New York street. Soon he'd learn everything about America and be a real American.

And there, coming closer and closer, was Ellis Island with its big sprawling building. In that building, their fate would be sealed. They'd be allowed to enter America or ordered back to Europe.

Two nights ago he'd overheard Anna and her friend, Rose Finkel, whispering in the darkness of the airless steerage cabin.

"Sometimes they send you back," said Rose. "Especially if you're sick. Especially if you have the eye sickness."

"We're not sick," said Anna.

"Some sicknesses you don't even know you have," said Rose. "It comes out in the inspection."

The way she whispered "inspection" made Joseph's heart skip a beat. It sounded like torture.

As if she'd read his mind, Rose continued, "The inspection is terrible."

No. No, Joseph thought. I can't go back to Russia. Joseph shuddered, remembering his encounter with the Russian soldier in the woods. He never wanted to feel that scared again. But no matter how hard he'd tried to convince himself that Rose was only spreading rumors, he could still hear her whispered warning as the ship drew near Ellis Island.

"Sometimes they send you back."

Chapter Two

The Chosen

"Next. Next. Next."

The words echoed through Joseph's head as he stood in line beside Anna. When would the lines end? When would they stop being crammed together like herrings in a jar?

The ferry to Ellis Island was bad enough. It had no toilets or air. Just people pressing so close, he could barely breathe.

And then, in this huge building on Ellis Island, there were more people. Old people with faces wrinkled like leather, mamas and papas hushing crying babies, and young people waiting to meet relatives they didn't even know.

Joseph could smell the fear in the building, a sour stifling smell like spoiled milk. But no matter how much he hated the smell or the feeling of being herded like cattle or tagged like baggage, returning to Russia would be worse.

Joseph glanced at Anna. She'd lost so much weight from seasickness, her brown dress hung loosely on her shoulders. Anna hadn't said a word since they stepped off the ferry. She just stood beside Joseph biting her nails. He knew she was scared. She always bit her nails when she was scared. Why did Rose Finkel have to frighten them with all her talk of being sent back? Even he couldn't shake the nervous rumbling in his stomach.

Only Rose didn't seem worried. As the line crawled, she jabbered on and on about her father and his job in a shirtwaist factory.

"Maybe he can help you find work

too, Anna," Rose offered. "He knows people in New York and he speaks English. He's been in New York since 1904, five years already," she told them for the third time.

"Next," barked the inspector, as they inched closer.

It was a young woman's turn.

"Name and who are you traveling with?" the inspector asked the woman in Yiddish.

"Manya Karetsky and I am alone," she answered.

"Who is meeting you?"

"My uncle Sol Karetsky," she answered.

A doctor quickly listened to Manya's heart and without a word, marked her with blue chalk and stuck a letter H around her neck.

"What is this?" Manya stammered.

"You may have a heart problem," said the doctor. "We will have to examine you more. We cannot admit you now."

"It must be a mistake," cried Manya.

"My uncle is waiting. I cannot stay here. Oh please. Let me go to my uncle. I am not sick."

But despite her tears and protests, the sobbing girl was led away.

Anna's face turned white as new snow, as Manya disappeared from sight.

"Next," barked the inspector.

It was Rose's turn.

"Name and who are you with?" the inspector asked.

Rose answered without hesitation.

Her health inspection proceeded easily till the sharp buttonhook pin was pushed under her eyelid.

"Ay. Ay," Rose winced in pain.

But when the inspector barked, "Next," her face burst into a relieved smile.

"Don't worry Anna," she whispered, squeezing Anna's hand warmly. "It will be fine for you too."

But Anna didn't seem to hear. She looked dazed, as if someone had hit her with a brick.

"Anna, move," Joseph nudged her.

As if hypnotized, Anna took a step forward.

"Name and who are you traveling with?" barked the inspector.

Anna said nothing.

"Name. Name," the inspector boomed impatiently.

But Anna was still silent.

Talk Anna, Joseph wanted to shout. Talk, or they'll send us back.

Suddenly the inspector lifted his hand to mark Anna with chalk. but before he could do anything, Joseph stepped hard on Anna's foot.

"Ouch," she cried. "What are you doing, Joseph?"

"So, you can talk," said the inspector. "For a minute, I thought you were slow or stupid. I almost marked you as having mental problems."

"I'm fine," said Anna, shaking her curly brown hair as if waking from sleep. "My name is Anna Wisotsky and I am traveling with my 10-year-old brother, Joseph."

It was finally Joseph's turn, but Joseph didn't wait for the inspector to speak. "My name is Joseph Wisotsky and I want to be an American," he announced.

"Well, Joseph Wisotsky," said the inspector, with a small smile, "welcome, but be careful where you step in America. It can be tough for a young boy like you."

"I will be careful," said Joseph, returning the smile, but he didn't really believe the inspector. This was the hard part, not America. America was exciting and full of adventure. "Ach," he groaned as the sharp buttonhook jabbed his eye. But then it was over.

Joseph turned to Anna and smiled. The golden doors to America were about to open and beckon them in.

Chapter Three

Aunt Sophie

"Joseph! Anna!"

They stood at the Kissing Post, the room where relatives were reunited. Amidst the shouts and tears of joy, the warm embraces and awkward first meetings, Joseph saw a short, round-faced woman wildly waving a photo in their direction.

"I am your Aunt Sophie!" she exclaimed, grabbing them both to her chest in a tight squeeze.

Could this really be Aunt Sophie? thought Joseph. She was much older than he'd imagined. He was sure she'd look like her picture, slender with masses of dark brown hair piled on her head like a crown. Not this plump woman with a mound of gray hair perched on her head like a noodle kugel.

"Thank God. Thank God," Aunt Sophie repeated over and over, wiping tears from her eyes . "My dear brother's children are finally here. Oh, how pale and thin you both are. And look at your clothes, so crumpled and worn. You must have slept in them. Are these three satchels all you have?"

Aunt Sophie talked so fast, she barely waited for an answer.

"How is my brother and your dear Mama?" she continued. "It has been 15 years since I saw them last. Fifteen years since my husband, Herschel, and I came to America. How happy Herschel would have been to meet you both. If only he had lived to see this day." Aunt Sophie dabbed her eyes again with a handkerchief as she hustled them onto another ferry.

This time, to Joseph's relief, there

was no more checking or inspections. This time, when they arrived on land, they were free to walk down the streets of New York.

"Come. We have a long walk home," said Aunt Sophie. "I am a little low on money this month. My boarders, the Blumbergs, owe me. So we must walk."

Everywhere Joseph looked there were people, pushcarts, horsecars, all mingling together like the potatoes and meat in Mama's Sabbath cholent stew. But not all the smells were as inviting as Mama's cholent. The stinky smells of horse manure, rotting garbage and sweating people all mixed with the delicious smells of pickles, garlic, roasted chestnuts, steaming sweet potatoes and spicy chickpeas.

Joseph looked up. The sun and sky seemed much farther away than in the shtetl. There were no trees or grass like at home, just brick buildings with zig-zaggedy metal sticking out from the windows.

"What are those?" he asked Aunt Sophie, pointing to the jagged structures.

"Fire escapes," she answered. "They're a way to leave a building in case of fire. And on hot nights, they're a place to go for a little air."

As soon as Joseph entered Aunt Sophie's building on Rivington Street he knew what she meant about air. A cool air blew in the street, but in the narrow halls of Aunt Sophie's building, the air was heavy with cigar smoke and the smell of overcooked cabbage.

"We are up on the third floor," said Aunt Sophie, huffing and puffing like a worn-out steam engine. "I rent out three of my rooms, but you're lucky, the small one is free this week. Next week, you will have to share. But next week is next week. Today a little cabbage soup is just what you need."

Oh, not cabbage soup! thought Joseph, as they reached the third floor. His nose was full of cabbage smells.

What if Aunt Sophie's cabbage soup tasted as bad as those smells?

"Eat. Eat. What are you waiting for?" asked Aunt Sophie, after they'd deposited their satchels in a tiny windowless room.

Joseph's stomach heaved as he stared at the limp chunks of cabbage floating in the yellow-gray broth.

"Eat. Eat," said Aunt Sophie again. "It's good and nourishing."

Joseph lifted his spoon and closed his eyes. With one gulp, he downed a spoonful of the cabbage soup.

"Oh," he murmured, for the soup was surprisingly good. It was almost as good as his mama's soup.

Suddenly hungry, Joseph ate another mouthful and then another.

"See? I told you it was good. My poor Herschel always said my soup was the best in New York," said Aunt Sophie, beaming. "So finish up. Then we will wash and tomorrow you will register for school."

"School?" said Joseph. He hadn't thought about school. "But I can't speak English. How can I go to school?"

"Most immigrants can't speak English," explained Aunt Sophie. "They will put you in a lower grade till you learn how to speak."

A lower grade? With little children? Joseph didn't like the sound of that at all.

Chapter Four

Sam

"Grade one!" protested Joseph to Anna, after his first day at school. "There are babies in that class. I am not going to school with babies. They don't even know how to wipe their own noses."

"But Joseph. It will not be forever. Just till you learn English. You're a fast learner. Papa always said you have a good head, not like that foolish Mendel in the shtetl."

"But this isn't the shtetl. I knew everything and everyone in the shtetl."

"Your teacher, Miss Williams, is nice," said Anna.

"Maybe she is," said Joseph, "but what does she know? She teaches babies." Joseph plunked down on the stoop of Aunt Sophie's building and stared at three boys playing catch in the street.

"I am going inside," said Anna. "My shoes are pinching my feet."

"I want to stay outside for awhile," said Joseph.

"Remember, supper is at six. Rose and her father are coming after supper. Her father has found a job for me at a shirtwaist factory."

"Don't worry. I'll be there," said Joseph. "I like Aunt Sophie's soup."

"Tonight she told me she's making knishes special for us," Anna told him.

"Mmm . . ." said Joseph, smacking his lips at the thought of knishes—creamy mashed potatoes and succulent fried onions all rolled into a package of dough. "Aunt Sophie talks a lot but she sure cooks good food."

Anna patted Joseph on the shoulder and hobbled inside.

Joseph stood up as soon as she left, but before he could hop off the step, a ball bounced hard into his chest. Startled, Joseph glared at the thin tall boy with cropped black hair who had thrown the ball.

"Gimme that ball," the boy barked in English.

Joseph didn't understand the boy's words, but from the boy's tone and sneer, Joseph knew he wasn't apologizing.

"Watch where you throw," said Joseph, throwing the boy back his ball.

"Watch where you sit, greenie," the boy snarled back, this time in Yiddish.

For a minute both boys stared at each other. Then Joseph's face broke out into a smile. "I am a greenie now," he told the boy, "but soon I'll be a regular American. I catch on to things fast."

Maybe it was the confidence in Joseph's' voice, or the sparkle in his

green eyes or his playful smile that Mama said could melt ice. Whatever it was, the tall thin boy smiled back at Joseph.

"My name is Sam," he said. "What's yours?"

"Joseph."

"Come on. Play catch with us, Joseph. And by the way, this is Al and Lou."

Joseph smiled at Sam's friends. Al was shorter than Sam with wavy brown bangs that half-covered his eyes while Lou's straight brown hair hung limply over his ears.

Al and Lou nodded. For the next hour and a half, the four played together. The conversation bounced back and forth between English and Yiddish and it didn't take long for Joseph to figure out a few words like "ball," "catch" and "stupid." Sam and his friends used "stupid" a lot, especially when someone missed a good throw.

Joseph was so absorbed in the game, he didn't even notice the sun set.

"Jo-seph!" a voice suddenly shrieked from upstairs. Joseph looked up.

Aunt Sophie was standing on the fire escape wearing an apron and waving a large wooden spoon. "Supper is ready," she called. "Come up and wash."

"I have to go," said Joseph.

"Meet us at the corner tomorrow at ten," said Sam.

"I can't," said Joseph. "I have to go to school."

"School? School is for babies," said Sam. "I don't go any more. Not since last year when I was twelve. We have better things to do with our time. Right boys?"

"Right," said Al and Lou, winking at each other.

"Jo-seph!" called Aunt Sophie again.

"I have to go now," said Joseph, and with a wave to his new friends, he ran up the stairs, two at a time.

Chapter Five

Watch Me

"So, how was baby school today?" Sam teased Joseph.

Sam teased Joseph about school every day and every day Joseph said, "Ah. Let's not talk about it. Let's play catch."

And for a few hours, before Aunt Sophie called Joseph for supper, the boys played ball. As they played, Joseph listened to the escapades of the older three. Most of the time, Sam talked. Joseph could tell that Sam was the leader and Al and Lou went along with his plans and ideas.

Sam told how they walked around streets where Irish, Chinese, Rumanians, Hungarians, even Gypsies lived. He talked about fishing in the East River and climbing rocks in Central Park. He described the subway, the new way to travel by underground train, faster than a bird through air.

It sounded like such fun to Joseph, more fun, for sure, than sitting in school with a bunch of first graders learning the alphabet.

"Who's that new man in your building?" Sam asked Joseph. "He looks mean."

"That's Mr. Plucknik and he is mean," said Joseph. "He's the new boarder and I have to share a room with him. Anna has moved into Aunt Sophie's room."

"Plucknik?" said Sam. "Plucknik. Clucknick. Like a chicken?"

"I wish he was a chicken," said Joseph. "A chicken wouldn't snore like thunder in my ear every night. A chicken wouldn't bark at me like a dog."

"Does your aunt like Mr. Plucknik?" asked Al.

"Aunt Sophie says it doesn't matter if she likes him or not. He pays on time and with two more mouths to feed, you can't be so choosy. Anna is making some money at the shirtwaist factory but it's not much. She's a beginner and they don't pay beginners much. I wish I had enough money to pay for a room just for Anna and me. At least Anna doesn't snore."

"Hey, Joseph," said Sam suddenly, "are you hungry?"

"I'm starving," said Joseph. "Since Mr. Plucknik's come, Anna and I get smaller portions. And Mr. Plucknik eats like a horse. Sometimes I get so hungry at night, my stomach rumbles as loud as Mr. Plucknik's snores."

"Come on then. Follow me," said Sam.

"Where?" asked Joseph.

"You'll see," said Sam, with a wink.

Joseph followed the boys down

Rivington Street to Delancey. Delancey was a sea of pushcarts filled with everything from garlicky pickles to a strange yellow fruit Joseph had never seen before.

'What's that?" he asked pointing to the long skinny fruit.

"Want a taste?" asked Sam.

"Is it good?" asked Joseph.

"It's like sunshine and sugar all rolled into one," said Sam.

"Really?" said Joseph. "But I have no money to buy it."

"You don't need money. Watch me," said Sam. And before Joseph knew it, Sam snatched the yellow fruit from under the pushcart owner's eyes.

"Go," Sam whispered under his breath to the boys.

Before the pushcart owner noticed, the four boys ran down the street. They ran all the way to Essex Street and then flopped down on a stoop.

"Here kid," said Sam, holding the fruit out for Joseph. "Eat and enjoy."

Joseph stared at the fruit. He wanted to taste it, but how could he eat stolen food?

"Come on, kid. Are you gonna be a real American or not?" said Sam, sensing Joseph's discomfort. "Sometimes you have to take the things you want in this city. Right, boys?"

"Right," said Al and Lou.

The fruit was so tempting and Joseph was so hungry. He only had a roll all day with half a glass of milk. Surely one taste of this fruit wouldn't be a sin.

"Maybe just this once," said Joseph. "It smells so good."

"It's called a banana," said Lou. Joseph was surprised to hear Lou speak up. Lou rarely spoke. He just looked at you with his big, sad, brown eyes. Sam said Lou's mother had died of diphtheria last month and he was taking it hard.

Joseph bit into the soft flesh of the banana. For a minute, he said nothing. He just chewed and swallowed, savoring every bite. "This is best thing I have tasted in my whole life," he said.

"I told you it was good," said Sam.

As Joseph munched the last piece of banana, he looked up. The sun was beginning to set. "I have to get home. Aunt Sophie will yell if I'm late."

All the way home, Joseph could smell the delicious banana on his fingers. But on Rivington Street, he passed a pushcart owner hunched wearily over a pile of shirts and pants and he thought about Papa. He knew what Papa would say: "It is wrong to steal Joseph, no matter what."

Chapter Six

Grade One

The second month at school was no better than the first. Joseph sat on the hard wooden bench in class trying to learn the sounds of the English letters. He was determined to learn quickly but English had such tricky sounds. Sometimes they refused to slide out of his mouth.

Worse than that, he had to sit in class with babies. Joseph was like a giant towering over the other first graders.

At recess he stood in a corner of the yard against the brick wall. He yearned to join the older boys in their stickball game but he couldn't approach them. What if they laughed and called him a baby or a greenie?

Joseph watched one group of boys toss a new boy's cap in the air, throwing it back and forth like a ball, as the new boy begged them to stop. They called him a stupid, know-nothing greenie till the boy burst into tears. A teacher led the sobbing boy inside as his tormentors snickered behind his back.

There was no way Joseph would let any of those boys make him cry. There was no way he wanted a teacher to lead him away as the kids laughed behind his back. It was better not to be noticed. It was better to learn English like an American and then ask to join the game.

After recess Joseph trudged back to class. As soon as he sat down, Miss Williams approached him. She looked at the letters he'd carefully written in his notebook earlier and smiled.

"Well done, Joseph. I wish all my

students learned as quickly as you. Perhaps you could help Avram with his letters? He has so much trouble, especially with G and R."

What could Joseph say? "Sure," he mumbled, looking over at Avram, one of the youngest and smallest of the boys in the class.

For the next two weeks, Joseph helped Avram every day. Avram was so happy, he followed Joseph outside every recess and stood beside him at the brick wall. Joseph wished he'd go away. What would the older boys think if they saw him hanging around with a first grade baby every day?

"Go play with your friends," Joseph told Avram, pointing to the grade one boys chasing each other around the yard.

"But you're my friend," said Avram, looking up at Joseph adoringly with his large almond-colored eyes. "You help me."

"I help you but I don't want to play with you. I'm too old to play with you."

But Avram smiled as if he hadn't heard a word and didn't budge from Joseph's side.

Joseph sighed. At least he wasn't stuck with babies after school. At least he had Sam, Al and Lou to play with every afternoon. By now, Joseph understood almost everything they were saying in English and he spoke a mixture of English and Yiddish back to them.

A week passed and Avram continued to glue himself to Joseph at recess. Joseph hated it more each day. Avram just stood there, not saying much, just looking up at Joseph as if Joseph was a King and Avram was his faithful servant. Joseph decided he had to tell Avram, clearly and firmly, to get lost on Monday.

But on Monday, before Joseph could say anything, Avram raced over to Joseph with a package wrapped in day-old newspaper. "For you," he said.

"What's this?" asked Joseph.

"A surprise," said Avram beaming.

Joseph unwrapped the package. Inside were a small cake, two apples and a banana.

"My mama sent it to thank you for teaching me," said Avram. "She is proud of how I make my G's and R's now. See?"

Avram wrote G and R in his notebook and held them up for Joseph to inspect. Joseph couldn't help smiling. They did look better now. They looked almost like the letters Miss Williams drew on the blackboard.

"Avram's really improved, thanks to you," said Miss Williams, walking over. "And your English has improved at the same time. You're speaking better every day, Joseph."

It was true. Joseph was feeling more confident each day and those strange English words were starting to roll off his tongue with ease.

"Do you like the cake?" asked Avram at recess.

"I didn't taste it yet," said Joseph.

"Taste it," implored Avram.

Joseph took a bite. "It's good. Here, have some." Then he broke off a chunk for Avram.

"Mmm," said Avram. "My mother makes the best cakes in the world, but she only makes them when she has enough money for butter and sugar. Sometimes she doesn't have enough money."

Joseph sighed. How could he tell Avram to scram now?

Joseph stared longingly as the older boys played ball. Soon, he told himself. Soon, I'll ask to play too.

After all, he was learning new words every day like "pushcart," "hurry up," "fire," "sidewalk," "bicycle," "walk," "rat," "dog" and "stink." The words piled up in his head. When he needed them, he pulled them out like rabbits from a magician's hat.

Even Aunt Sophie noticed how much Joseph was improving.

"Maybe you'll get a job after school

now and help me out with expenses," she suggested.

A job? Joseph hadn't thought about a job. He'd seen boys his age deliver newspapers or carry shirtwaists from factories to stores. But how could he find a job?

He asked Sam, "What do you think?" But instead of an answer, Sam burst into laughter.

"What's so funny?" asked Joseph.

"You're still such a greenie. Who'd hire you? They'll laugh in your face," said Sam.

"No. They won't," protested Joseph, but he wasn't sure. What if Sam was right?

Chapter Seven

Joe, Not Joseph

Two cold winter months passed. Joseph shivered in his thin coat as he walked to school each day. And each day he thought about asking the boys his age if he could play with them at recess. But with Avram glued to his side, it was hard to approach the older boys.

Then on a Monday, early in January of the new year, 1910, Avram was home, sick.

Today I will ask to join the game, Joseph decided as he wrote in his notebook. My English is surely good enough now.

So as soon as recess began, Joseph approached a group of four boys. "I would like to play too," he said smiling. The boys weren't impressed with Joseph's words or smiles. They ignored him.

"I would like to join your game," Joseph repeated louder.

"Aren't you in grade one?" sneered one of the boys.

"Yes," said Joseph. "But before he could explain that it was only for a little while, the sneering boy said, "Then you must be stupid."

"I'm not stupid," Joseph protested. "I am only in grade one till I learn a little more English."

"Well you talk English good enough for me," said another one of the group. "I think you're in grade one because you're stupid."

"Yes, stupid," all four boys chanted. "Stupid! Stupid! Stupid!"

Joseph's face turned red as a cooked beet. He wished he hadn't approached those boys. He wished he'd just stayed in his safe corner where no one bothered him.

Joseph walked to the other end of the yard, far away from the group of chanting, sneering boys. But he couldn't escape the sound of their laughter ringing in his ears.

There was no way he would approach them again while he was stuck in grade one. But how long would that be? What if he was left in grade one for the rest of the year? There was a boy in another class who had stayed in grade one for two years and he was already eleven.

At least I have Sam, Al and Lou to play with, thought Joseph. They like me and they're not babies. They're even older than those boys in the yard and they know everything about America.

Joseph played with them every day, even when it snowed. But on snowy days, instead of catch, they tossed snowballs at each other, at brick tenement walls, or at passing carriages.

"Hey, Joseph," said Sam later that afternoon. "Joseph is a name for a greenie. A real American needs an American name. Call yourself Joe instead."

"Joe!" said Joseph, trying the name on like a pair of new pants. "I like that. It sounds like a real American. From today on, just call me Joe!"

"Good," said Sam.

"So where are Lou and Al?" asked Joe.

"Lou's father is making him work at the hat factory where his father works. His father says he'll throw him out on the street unless he works," explained Sam. "And Al is sick with fever. But let's not think about them now. Let's have an adventure. Skip that baby school tomorrow and we'll take the subway uptown."

It wasn't the first time Sam had suggested Joe skip school but it was the first time he'd offered Joe such an exciting adventure. The subway! Uptown! Sam had told Joe all about it. The subway was like a whole city underground, Sam explained.

And Uptown was where the rich lived in beautiful mansions with many servants. How could he resist the chance to go, especially after the awful time he had at recess? How could he resist after spending another miserable night with Mr. Plucknik?

Aside from Mr. Plucknik's snoring and barking, Mr. Plucknik was a pig. He left dirty clothes all over the tiny room he shared with Joe and regularly dumped his smelly shirts and socks on Joe's cot. Joe hated it. He could smell Mr. Plucknik's stinky socks and shirts even in his dreams.

"Aunt Sophie," Joe begged. "Could I please move in with you and Anna? I hate Mr. Plucknik."

"There's barely room for Anna in my room," said Aunt Sophie impatiently. "What do you think? I like Mr. Plucknik?

But he pays and that's good enough for me."

Sometimes Aunt Sophie sounded so angry, especially when she talked about money. Joe often saw her count out coins late at night from a tin can she kept hidden in her room. Joe knew he and Anna were an extra burden to her. He knew Aunt Sophie worried constantly that she wouldn't have enough money to feed and clothe them. If only she didn't bark so much. It made him feel like she was sorry they came.

But when she suddenly hugged him or baked her special honey cake with raisins just because he liked it, Joe knew she was glad they came. Or when he overheard her tell Mrs. Klein from the first floor about her lovely Anna who was "so sweet and talented with a needle" and her clever Joseph, "smart as a scholar," then he was sure she wanted them there.

If only Mr. Plucknik would be captured by a band of Gypsies or move to Philadelphia where his sister lived. Then things would be much better. But Joe was sure that Mr. Plucknik was so irritating that not even his sister or the Gypsies would want him.

Still, even with Aunt Sophie's barking, and being stuck with grade one babies day after day and even sharing a room with stinky Plucknik, there was no way Joe wanted to go back to Russia.

You couldn't travel freely in Russia as a Jew. You couldn't explore what lay beyond your shtetl. But in America, you could go anywhere without being questioned or stopped. And in America, soldiers didn't threaten to kill you in the woods or burn your house down.

Anna didn't feel the way he did. She hated New York. In Russia, she used to tell him funny stories about hairy creatures who lived in trees and she always sang around the house as she helped Mama cook and clean.

But all that changed since they arrived in New York. Anna had no more time for stories or songs. Her eyes were often filled with tears.

"My boss is a tyrant, just like the Czar back in Russia," she told Joe. "He forces us to work faster and faster and if we spend more than five minutes in the bathroom, he screams we are wasting time and threatens to reduce our already small pay. Is this what we left Russia for? Endless work and little to show for it but tired bones. I want to go home to Mama and Papa. There's no gold in New York, just misery."

"But Anna, it's just the beginning," said Joseph. "It will get better."

"When?" asked Anna. "When?" and Joseph had no answer.

Chapter Eight

Uptown

Joe felt like a thief sneaking out of the house to meet Sam. He knew Anna would be upset that he was skipping school. She'd remind him how heart-broken Mama and Papa would be. She'd tell him how important it was to go to school and learn. But he'd only skip school for one day. One day to see what lay beyond Rivington and Delancey. One day to go somewhere special.

He wished he hadn't told Anna about his new name last night. He knew she was determined to write Mama and Papa about returning to Russia and when he said, "Don't call me Joseph anymore. Call me Joe," she'd burst into tears.

"See how this terrible place has changed you?" she'd cried. "You speak English all the time and hardly any Yiddish. And now you want to change your name. Mama and Papa gave you the name Joseph and now you want to throw it away like an old hat. You are not the same Joseph who left home but a hoodlum who plays on the street with other hoodlums. Oh, how I hate this New York."

"I'm not a hoodlum," Joe had shouted back. "And I like New York!" Then he'd run to his room only to be greeted by a monstrous snore from the sleeping Mr. Plucknik.

Joe sat on his bed watching Mr. Plucknik's enormous hairy chest rise and fall like a stormy ocean wave and for a minute, even Joe wished he was back with his parents in Russia.

But that was yesterday, Joe told himself. Today the sun warmed his face. Today there was no Mr. Plucknik or Anna to make him feel terrible. Today he was going to have a great adventure.

"Ready?" said Sam.

"Ready," said Joe.

"Then let's go!"

"But I have no money for tickets," said Joe.

"You don't need money. Just do as I do and move fast," said Sam.

The boys walked past the crowds of people and pushcarts on Rivington Street to the El, the train that traveled above the street.

"Make yourself invisible," whispered Sam. Joe followed Sam's lead as he melted into the crush of people at the station. Soon they snuck on the train without paying.

"But why did we go downtown?" asked Joe, as they ran off the El.

"To get to the subway on Canal Street. Then from there it's uptown to 59th Street and the park. And here it is—

The Subway!" Sam announced it, as if they'd reached the entrance to a new world.

And it was a new world. An underground world of wooden ticket booths, glistening tiles and graceful columns. But most of all it was a world where trains rumbled through dark mysterious tunnels deep in the belly of the city.

"Remember, invisible!" whispered Sam as he led Joe into the thick of the crowd. And somehow, again, they squeezed onto the train without paying a cent.

As the train zoomed through the tunnels, Joe and Sam pressed their faces to the windows, trying to catch a glimpse of what lay on the tracks, but it was too dark to see anything but shadows.

"Next stop, 59th Street!" Sam sang like a conductor.

Joe's heart raced with excitement. Uptown! Soon he'd see it. Soon he'd stroll around Uptown streets like a rich man. In America you could do that!

And Uptown was as wonderful as Joe imagined. Mansions lined wide streets. Men in dark suits and bowler hats hurried to work. Women in taffeta and velvet with large flowered hats strolled and shopped.

It was so different from Rivington Street. Here there was room to breathe. Here there was space to walk. And beyond each carved wooden door, Joseph pictured sumptuous breakfasts of fresh eggs, warm bread, hot coffee, rich cream, all being served in endless quantity.

Joe wished he could describe it to Anna, but he couldn't, of course. He even wished he could tell Miss Williams, who always took time to compliment him on his improving English. But there was no way he could tell her either. He already had to make up a story about missing school.

Still it was fun to be away from school.

It was good to be away from the back wall at recess beside Avram. It was good not to face those boys who wouldn't let him play.

But what was he going to do about tomorrow? Sam wanted to take him to Central Park tomorrow. "We'll climb rocks like explorers and watch the skaters twirl on the lake. Central Park is like your woods behind the shtetl. You'll love it," Sam said.

Sam was right. Joe loved the woods. Until the day the Russian soldier had almost killed him, the woods had been his favorite place. He used to take a chunk of bread and sit on a log in the woods, imagining Anna's hairy creatures hiding in the trees. He'd listen to birds and watch rabbits and squirrels scurrying around. He'd throw pebbles into the small brook and watch them dance across the water. Sometimes he'd even catch a small fish.

But from the day the soldier threatened him, Joe never went to the woods again. He only dreamed about it. And now he had a chance to explore New York woods in Central Park, all only a subway ride away.

He had to go there. At least once.

"I'll be here on the stoop waiting in the morning," said Sam.

Joe ran up the steps to his building. He could smell chicken soup in the hall and on the stairs. It was coming from their apartment. He hoped Aunt Sophie had made the soup with kreplach, meat and onions wrapped in dough. One thing for sure about Aunt Sophie, she could turn a little meat and onions into magic.

Hurrah! Aunt Sophie had made kreplach! "So how was school today?" asked Aunt Sophie, as she puttered in the kitchen. "How is your English? Are you listening to the teacher?"

"Everything's fine," said Joe. "And my English is getting better each day."

"Good," said Aunt Sophie. "Your parents would be happy to know you are working hard at school." Then she yammered on about the price of chicken and beef and how much her feet hurt from so much walking to get the best prices. "If you don't watch those butchers, they rob you blind," she lamented.

Joe nodded. It was always about money.

"I'm totally worn out," said Aunt Sophie. "I'm going to sleep early. Wash up, Joseph, and then get some sleep too. A growing boy like you needs rest."

Joe went to his room. As usual, Mr. Plucknik was asleep early and, as usual, he was snoring like thunder. For a long time, Joe lay on his bed imagining Central Park. Then he heard the click of shoes on the floor. Anna was home. Suddenly, he heard glass shatter and then the sound of sobs coming from the kitchen.

Joe slipped out of bed. Anna was picking up broken shards of glass from the linoleum floor. Tears were dribbling

down her cheeks and her face was red from crying. Joe leaned over to help.

"Thank you," said Anna in a choked voice. "I don't know how it happened. The cup just fell out of my hand. It's been such a terrible day and now, on top of everything, I have to buy Aunt Sophie a new cup. I barely have enough money to pay our rent."

"Maybe she'll understand and not ask you to pay," said Joe.

"Aunt Sophie?" Anna said sniffing. "You know how she is about money and I can't blame her. It is so hard to have enough money to live in New York. But it's more than that. My friend Lucy was fired today. The boss complained that she takes too long to finish her work. I tried to explain that Lucy takes care of her old grandmother and two young sisters. I tried to tell him that Lucy is a good worker but sometimes she is a little tired after helping her family. But the boss just gave me an angry stare and yelled at me to be quiet and not interfere in what I don't know. Then he told Lucy to pack up and leave. Lucy grabbed my hand and whispered, "Thank you for trying to help," and then she walked out.

"She'll find another job. I heard they are always looking for workers," said Joe.

"But all the bosses are the same in all the factories. I hate them. Today it's Lucy. Tomorrow it could be me or someone else. They treat us like the slaves. When I helped Mama and Papa with their work, they treated me with respect. I miss them. I want to go back to Russia."

"But Russia is full of Cossacks, Anna," said Joe. "Remember what they did to our cousins? Remember what almost happened to me? And remember, Mama and Papa want to come to America too."

"It may take years for them to save enough money and meanwhile, I will be too tired and sick to care about anything. There is no hope for a future here."

"But ... but," protested Joe.

"Go to sleep, Joseph," Anna said. "It is no use to talk any more. I am too weary for words. Tomorrow it all starts again. The work. The bosses, the orders and this time I will be working without my dear friend, Lucy, by my side. You don't know how much it helped to share a smile with her and now even that small pleasure is gone."

Anna lifted herself wearily from the chair and stumbled into the dark room she shared with Aunt Sophie.

Back in his bed, Joe lay awake thinking.

"If I have to leave New York, I have to see Central Park before I go. I just have to."

Then Joe fell asleep, dreaming of forests and tiny, magical creatures who lived in the heart of trees.

Chapter Nine

The Park

"Hey! Where do you think you two are going?" shouted the man in the ticket booth as Joe and Sam skittered past him onto the El.

Joe and Sam didn't respond but squeezed themselves into the crowd of workers. Luckily the platform was so full of people and noise, the shouts from the man in the booth were drowned out.

But it was close. Joe's heart beat wildly under his shirt. He was sure the woman beside him could hear it pound too.

"Phew," he whispered to Sam, when the train finally began to move.

"You think that was close," said Sam. "Once a ticket booth man grabbed me by my hair and yanked me off the platform. When he wasn't looking, I snuck back on. It's all part of the fun. Look Joe, the sun is coming out. Wait till you see Central Park in the sun. You'll love it."

Sam was right. Snow sparkled on thc trees like lace on a dress as they walked to the lake. They stood at the edge of the frozen lake watching skaters glide on the ice. Some were as graceful as dancers but others stumbled and fell like clowns.

"I wish I had skates," said Joe.

"Not me," said Sam. "You could break a bone or something on that ice. I just like to watch. But come on, I want to show you my favorite place."

Joe followed Sam deeper and deeper into the park. There were few people in this part of the park. It was quiet and peaceful like the woods. Joe felt far away from the bustle and noise of the city.

"Here we are," said Sam, pointing to a group of large jagged boulders. "From the top you can see all of Manhattan. Come on."

The rocks were slippery with snow but the boys soon clambered to the top. And just as Sam said, they could see far across the city. The buildings in the distance glistened like jewels.

For a minute Joe closed his eyes, imagining the rocks in spring and summer. What a perfect spot to bring a chunk of bread, listen to birds and watch squirrels.

There was nobody to bother them here. No one to chase them away. Central Park belonged to them as well as to anyone in New York. But when Joe opened his eyes, two older boys were climbing the rocks. Both were tall and as burly and muscular as boxers. They scowled at Joe and Sam when they reached the top.

"Get out of here," one barked at them. "These are our rocks."

"These rocks don't belong to anyone," said Sam.

"They're ours. We've claimed them," snarled the other boy.

"Come on," said Joe, in a friendly voice. "We can all share the rocks."

But Joe's friendly gesture only seemed to anger the boys more. "Get off or we'll throw you off," they shouted. Then the tallest boy shoved Joe so hard, he fell on his knees against a sharp rock. The rock cut through his pants like a knife.

"S ... Sam!" Joe called, but there was no answer. Despite the searing pain in his legs, Joe quickly steadied himself and scuttled off the rocks. As he ran, he scanned the surrounding bushes, trees and path for Sam, but he couldn't see him anywhere. Where was he?

There was no time now to think about it. He had to get out of this part of the park, but which way should he go? Joe took a deep breath, desperately trying to decide which way to go, when he heard a voice.

"Psst ..." it said.

Joe looked up. A figure was hiding behind a bush. It was Sam!

"Where were you?" asked Joe. "Those two almost made me break my neck."

"There was no point in both of us getting hurt," said Sam.

"But you left me. I don't know my way around the park."

"Don't make such a big deal about it. You're fine, aren't you? I knew you could handle yourself. See? No harm done."

Joe didn't know what to say. His heart was still pounding. His leg was still throbbing. How could Sam leave him to face those boys alone?

"Come on," said Sam, smiling as if nothing had happened. "Are you hungry?"

Joe sighed. What could he do? Maybe Sam didn't really mean to put him in danger. "I'm starved," said Joe, "but I don't have a cent."

"You don't need a cent. I told you, in New York you can always find a way to get some money. Watch me and learn."

Sam and Joe passed a bench. A well-dressed older man was napping on the bench. Sam quietly approached him and smoothly lifted his wallet from his coat pocket. Joe knew from Sam's swift sure movements that Sam had lifted wallets before.

"One dollar!" Sam whispered as he emptied the man's soft leather wallet. "See? It's not hard. Your turn next."

"I can't," said Joe.

"What's the matter with you? Look at this man's expensive clothes. He won't miss the money. You're not in the shtetl anymore, Joe. Let's eat something and then maybe you'll get smart."

"I'm not that hungry any more," said Joe.

"Well I am," said Sam. "So let's go."

Joe followed Sam out of the park. Sam made everything sound so reasonable, even things Joe knew were wrong. Joe knew what his father would say: "Have you forgotten everything we taught you?" He could almost see the look of disappointment in his father's tired eyes as Sam led them out of the park and down a side street.

Joe followed Sam into the warmth of a small bakery. The intoxicating aroma of freshly baked bread hit Joe's nose like perfume. Joe's stomach growled as he eyed the breads, cookies and cakes neatly arranged behind glass.

"Not hungry, my foot," said Sam. "You'd love some nice warm bread. Come on. Tell the truth."

"You're right," said Joe. "I would."

"Four of those round rolls," Sam told the girl behind the counter as confidently as a rich man.

Then he handed two of the rolls to Joe. "I'll treat you today, but tomorrow it's your turn. See? A little money in your pocket makes you feel like Rockefeller and who did we hurt? Some rich man who has lots of money? Some rich man whose belly is full? Nah. He won't miss the money for a minute."

Joe bit into the roll. It tasted warm and buttery, but no matter how good it tasted, Joe felt an ache in his stomach when he thought of lifting a wallet from a man's pocket.

"Come on," said Sam, as if reading Joe's mind. "You'll see it's easy once you give it a try, but wait till tomorrow. Tomorrow we'll cross Brooklyn Bridge. Your eyes will pop out of your head when you see the bridge. It's the most beautiful bridge in the world."

"I'd better go back to school tomorrow, Sam. Miss Williams will get suspicious if I'm out too many days. She might tell Aunt Sophie and then I'll get in trouble."

"Who cares if your dumb aunt is mad or that baby teacher is suspicious," said Sam impatiently. "Tell the teacher you were sick. You're not too chicken to say that, are you?"

"No. I just can't tomorrow," Joe insisted.

Sam grunted and rolled his eyes. "So go back to that baby school. What do I care? You'll soon be desperate to get out and have an adventure. Anyway, I need to see how Al is doing. He's probably feeling much better by now and itching to make some real money. Al is one person who knows what's what. Al is a real American."

Chapter Ten

Sea Fever

Joe tried to shake off the memory of Sam's sneering tone as he climbed the stairs to his apartment. He tried to forget how scared he felt being pushed off the rocks in the park and abandoned by Sam. He tried to think about what excuse he was going to give Miss Williams for missing two days of school. He knew he'd better think fast, but he was so tired from the day, his head felt like it was stuffed with rags. *I'll think of something in the morning,* he decided.

But the next morning, as he waited

for Miss Williams to call his name for attendance, his mind was as blank as the blackboard.

"Joseph Wisotsky," she said in her soft firm voice.

"Here," said Joe.

"Where were you for the last two days?" she asked.

"I ... I ... was sick," stammered Joe.

"You certainly look well today," said Miss Williams, with a knowing look in her eyes. "Please see me at lunch."

Oh no! thought Joe. She knows! Would she tell Anna? Would she tell Aunt Sophie? Would she send him to Mr. Cutler, the principal? Would Mr. Cutler smack his hand with a stick for misbehaving?

All through class Joe worried about Miss Williams, as he stood against the wall with Avram, glued to his side, at recess.

"Are you feeling better today?" Avram asked him. "Did you have a fever? Were you coughing? My sister has a fever and my mama is worried about her."

"I'm fine," yelled Joe. "Stop asking me so much."

Avram's eyes filled with tears at Joe's angry tone. Joe wished he hadn't yelled at Avram, but why did Avram have to hang around him all the time?

At lunch, Joe strode over to Miss Williams desk, bracing himself for his punishment.

But instead of a lecture or a trip to Mr. Cutler, Miss Williams handed him a soft leather book with gilded pages. Joe had never held such a fine book before.

"Turn to page ten," she said. "Read the first stanza of the poem for me, please."

Joe stared at the poem. "It's hard," he said.

"Try it," insisted Miss Williams.

Joe took a deep breath. "Sea Fever," began Joe. As he read, he stumbled over many words like a drunken

sailor, but each time, Miss Williams helped him. By the third try, he read the first stanza with only a few mistakes.

"Tomorrow, I'd like you to read the first stanza in front of the class," she said.

"I can't," said Joe.

"You can," said Miss Williams. "Take this book home with you and practice."

"But it's your book," said Joe, noticing Miss Williams name in the inside of the front cover. Miss Williams had never loaned a book to another student in his class before.

"I know you will take good care of it," said Miss Williams, smiling.

Joe blushed. "Thank you," he said, tucking the book deep into his satchel. There was no way he would let Sam catch him with a book of poems. Sam would only laugh. "What kind of boy reads poetry like a girl?" he'd snicker.

But no matter what Sam thought, Joe liked the poem. He liked how the poet, John Masefield, wrote, "I must go down to the sea again, to the lonely sea and the sky." Joe remembered how when they sailed to America, on a gray day the sea had looked lonely and cold. And he knew what Mr. Masefield meant when he wrote, "And all I ask is a tall ship and a star to steer her by." On a clear night when the sea had been still as a pond and the stars glittered like gems, Joe had looked up, dreaming of what lay ahead.

"I'd better go inside," Joe told Sam that evening after they'd played ball for awhile. "I have a lot of homework."

"Don't you know that baby stuff yet?" said Sam. "Skip the homework. Tell the teacher you're sick again. Tell her your sickness came back. Come with me tomorrow. We'll walk across Brooklyn Bridge. It's the most amazing bridge in the world and you can see the whole city from it."

Joe sighed. Sam made it sound wonderful. Sam made everything sound wonderful and Uptown, the subway and Central Park had been wonderful. But what about Miss Williams? She trusted him with her beautiful book. She counted on him to read the poem.

"I can't," said Joe.

"Look, I'll even treat you to hot cocoa at this candy store I know in Brooklyn. I have a little money left over from that man on the bench."

"I can't. Not tomorrow," Joe said, heading inside.

"Well, I may not want to go another time," Sam called after him angrily. "Al is feeling better and we have plans. Big plans. Plans to make real money. We probably won't have time to play catch any more. So you'd better decide if you're with us or not. You're still a greenie, you know. No real American wants to be with a greenie." The threatening tone in Sam's voice reminded Joe of their first meeting.

"Give me your answer tomorrow," yelled Sam as Joe ran upstairs.

Before Joe could escape into his room, Aunt Sophie stopped him at the door. “Supper in ten minutes,” she said. “It is just you and me tonight. Anna is out and Mr. Plucknik ate early. But we only have the kitchen till seven. I promised the Blumbergs they could use it later.”

“Where is Anna?” Joe asked.

“She is attending some meeting about work. She said she would be out late and not to wait up. That girl works too hard. It would break your mother's heart to see how pale and thin she has become, like a ghost.”

It was true. Anna looked more and more tired every day. She bit her nails all the time and her fingers were red and raw from biting and pricking her fingers with the needles she sewed with at work. Joe wished he could make some money so Anna didn't have to work day and night. He wished he had some money so he could move out of the room with Mr. Plucknik. But how could he get money?

He knew what Sam wanted him to do. Joe was sure that Sam's hints about making money had to do with stealing. And Joe was sure from Sam's tone that this time, if Joe didn't go along, Sam and Al would never be friends with him again. And without them, who would be his friends? Not Avram for sure. Not those babies in his class either. And certainly not those older boys at school who'd made fun of him. What was he going to do? It was lonely without friends.

"Sup-per!" called Aunt Sophie.

"Coming," said Joe and he plunked down at the battered wooden table for boiled potatoes in a beet soup called borscht and two slices of rye bread.

"How's the borscht?" asked Aunt Sophie, as he sipped a spoonful.

"Good," said Joe.

"I walked five long blocks to buy fresh beets," said Aunt Sophie. "If prices keep going up, I don't know what I'll do. I won't be able to afford anything but stale bread."

There it was again. The worry about money. Aunt Sophie worried constantly. She complained that the Blumbergs paid late. Only Mr. Plucknik, she said, paid on time.

As Aunt Sophie droned on about the price of food, all Joe could think about were Sam's angry words, "Are you with us or not? Give me your answer tomorrow."

Chapter Eleven

The Decision

All through supper, Joe worried about his decision. Part of him couldn't wait to leap into a new adventure and escape from the hard wooden benches at school and Avram's constant company at recess. And it was true. It would feel so good to have a pocket full of money. "Here, Aunt Sophie," he'd say, handing her a month's rent for the room. "Tell that stinky Plucknik to pack up his dirty clothes and go." Joe imagined his room without Plucknik. It would almost feel like a palace!

But how could he steal? "A good

person is worth more than gold," Mama always said. "Only money honestly earned can be honestly enjoyed," Papa always said. And then there were Anna and Aunt Sophie. If Aunt Sophie found out he was stealing, she'd toss him into the street. She'd call him a gonif, a thief, and never speak to him again. And if he was caught by the police, they'd throw him in jail or in a home for delinquent boys. Joe pictured himself being dragged to jail and he shuddered.

And what about Miss Williams and the poem? Joe dug into his satchel for the poetry book. It was so soft and beautiful. He read "Sea Fever" aloud again. Each time he loved the words more. They were like music. And each time, the words flowed more easily from his lips.

Oh, it was impossible to know what to do. His head hurt thinking about it.

"Joseph, please get my shawl from my room," said Aunt Sophie, "I feel a draft on my shoulders."

Joseph ran into the room Aunt Sophie shared with Anna. Everything was neatly arranged in the cramped room except for a letter lying on Anna's bed. Joe glanced at the letter. It was addressed to their parents! What was Anna writing? What was Anna planning? He had to know.

Joseph picked the letter up and read:

Dear Mama and Papa,

I know how hard you have worked to pay for our passage to America. I know you are saving money to join us, but I beg you to reconsider.

New York streets are not paved with gold but with misery, sweat and dirt. Although I have work, it is brutal work, long hours hunched over a table with no relief and all for little pay.

Aunt Sophie has little money and must take in boarders. There is little air in our rooms and everything is a struggle.

I am so miserable here and see

no future for myself. Joseph has learned English, but Joseph has changed so much since we came.

That's where the letter ended. Joe put it down and slumped on Anna's bed. What else was Anna going to say about him? Would she mention his friends? Would she tell their parents how he changed his name?

"Jo-seph!" called Aunt Sophie. "Where are you?"

Quickly Joseph grabbed Aunt Sophie's shawl draped over a chair and ran back to the kitchen.

"What took you so long?" asked Aunt Sophie.

"I ... I ... " Joe stammered, but Aunt Sophie, as usual, was so busy talking she hardly heard his response.

"Ah," she said, wrapping the shawl around her shoulders. "That's much better. I must be coming down with a cold. Would you like some tea and strudel? I made it special."

Joe nodded yes and bit into the warm strudel. Strudel was one of Aunt Sophie's specialties but tonight his stomach was in such a knot, he could barely enjoy it.

"What's the matter with you tonight?" said Aunt Sophie as he picked at the apple and raisin filling. "Isn't the strudel good?"

"It's delicious," said Joe. "I just have a stomachache."

"Did those hoodlums you hang around with give you something bad to eat? I tell you those boys are up to no good. That big one, Sam, has a bad look on his face."

"No," said Joe. "It's nothing like that. I'm just tired."

"Go ahead. Rest. I'll clean this up by myself." Aunt Sophie sighed as if she had a heavy load on her shoulders.

Joe threw himself on his cot. His head felt like it weighed a hundred pounds. He could barely keep his eyes open. Mr. Plucknik was snoring as always, but tonight Joe was so tired, the sound felt like it was coming from far, far away.

A loud knock on the door woke him. It was Aunt Sophie.

"Joseph, get up. You'll be late for school."

Oh no! Morning! He'd slept in his clothes. There was no time to change now. Joe leaped out of bed, ran to the kitchen, splashed cold water on his face, grabbed his satchel and raced down the stairs.

And there they were, Sam and Al. They were waiting on the front stoop for his answer, just like Sam said they would.

"Well," said Sam. "Are you ready to be part of our gang? Are you ready to fill your pockets with money? Are you ready to buy a new cap and look like a real American?"

"I ... I ... can't," said Joe.

"Why not?" Sam said, a hard, angry edge in his voice. "What's the matter with you? Are you still a stupid greenie?

Are you still too scared to become a real American? Do you want to be stuck with babies all your life in that stupid school reading useless books?" snarled Sam, grabbing Joe's satchel off his shoulder.

"Hey! Let go!" Joe yelled.

"Why? What's in here that's so special?" Sam sneered, opening the satchel. "A small pencil. A notebook, a book of ... poems? Look at this, Al. This greenie reads poems like a girl." Sam and Al howled with laughter.

"Give it back," said Joe. "Give it back or else."

"Or else what?" said Sam, beginning to tip the contents of the satchel into the slushy snow. But just before the book hit the soggy ground, Joe stepped hard on Sam's foot and yanked back his satchel.

"What did you do that for, you stupid greenie?" Sam wailed.

"Don't touch my things," said Joe, staring at Sam.

"Don't tell me what to do," said Sam and he raised his fist and smashed it into Joe's cheek.

Joe lurched toward the ground, but he didn't fall. His cheek burned like fire, his heart pounded with anger and hurt, but he pulled himself up. Silently he picked up his wet pencil and notebook, rubbed them on his pants and turned to go.

"Go rot in that stupid school," Sam shouted after him. "C'mon Al. Let's you and me make some real money."

And without another word, Sam and Al took off.

As soon as they were out of sight, Joe ran. His heart was still pounding but he had to get to school. Cradling his satchel like a baby in his arms, Joe ran till he reached his school.

Breathlessly, he slid into his seat, just as Miss Williams walked in.

"Joe, would you please come up and read for us?" she asked after attendance.

As Joe walked to the front of the room, he saw Miss Williams stare at the red bruise on his face, but she said nothing.

"'Sea Fever' by John Masefield," he began.

By the second sentence, Joe glanced up and when he did, his knees almost buckled. There, in the back of the class, stood Mr. Cutler, the principal, listening to every word.

Joe read on and despite the searing pain in his face and his shaky knees, he didn't stumble over a word.

"Well," said Mr. Cutler to Miss Williams, when he finished. "I agree something must be done. Come with me, Joseph."

No! No! Joe wanted to scream. I didn't do anything. I only cut school twice. Why am I in trouble?

Joe followed Mr. Cutler down the long dim hall, but they didn't stop at the principal's office. Mr. Cutler walked past his office and turned down

another hall till they reached the stairs. Then, Mr. Cutler walked up the stairs to the second floor and down another long dark hallway. Joe's heart beat faster with each step.

Where were they going?

Suddenly, Mr. Cutler stopped in front of a closed door. He knocked and the door opened.

"Good morning Miss O'Grady," he said to a gray-haired woman inside. "I have a new pupil for your fourth grade class. This is Joseph Wisotsky. He's a good reader and a fast learner."

And with that, Joe entered grade four.

Chapter Twelve

All Mixed Up

As soon as school was over, Joe ran home. He couldn't wait to tell Anna and Aunt Sophie what had happened at school. But halfway there, he saw Sam and Al hovering near a fruit pushcart and Joe quickly turned down an alley to avoid them.

It was still hard to believe that Sam had actually hit him in the face. How could Sam treat a friend like that? Sam had been nice to buy him the rolls near Central Park, show him Uptown and take him on the subway, but he'd abandoned him in the park to face those bullies alone. How could he be so mean? Wasn't Joe his friend? Didn't they have fun playing ball together and laughing? Sam was Joe's first American friend, but how could Sam really care about him if he hit him?

Everything was so mixed up. How could you feel angry and hurt and happy all at the same time? Why did bad things happen with good so you didn't know how to feel?

One thing he knew. He might as well tell Aunt Sophie and Anna about his face. They'd be pleased he was no longer hanging around with that "hoodlum bunch" as Anna and Aunt Sophie called them.

A sudden wave of relief washed over him. He winced every time he remembered how Sam had dumped his things out on the ground and taunted and hit him. He didn't want to be around anyone who treated him like that again.

Joe passed the hunched man selling shirts and pants from his pushcart.

The man who reminded him of Papa. Papa would be proud of him for standing up to Sam and for reading in front of the class. Papa and Mama would be proud at how quickly Joe had learned English.

He smiled as he remembered Miss Williams' words when he returned her book at the end of the day.

"I was proud of the way you read, Joseph," she'd said. "Does your face hurt very much?"

"Not that much," he'd answered, and it was true. He was feeling so happy about grade four, the pain hardly mattered. Only the memory of what Sam did hurt. It hurt more than his face.

Miss Williams nodded like she understood.

"Thanks for everything," said Joe, feeling suddenly shy with Miss Williams. He wished she were still his teacher. Miss O'Grady was okay but she hardly smiled. She didn't make you feel like you were someone special.

A block from the apartment, Joe passed Yossi's Knish Store. It had just opened. He stared at the window where a "Delivery Boy Wanted" sign hung. He breathed in the warm smells of baking dough, meat and potatoes wafting out from the store. Maybe he could ask them for a job. Imagine! If he delivered knishes, maybe they'd let him have samples. He could give some to Aunt Sophie, Anna, Avram, even Miss Williams. Sol, a boy in his new fourth grade class told Joe he had a job at a bakery and was allowed to take home two-day-old bread for free. Joe smacked his lips at the prospect of warm knishes.

Joe turned down his block. He scanned the street, wondering if Sam and Al were waiting on the stoop, ready to confront him. What would he say to them? How should he behave around them? What if they hit him again?

He wished he didn't have to face them. At least not today. But if he did, he wouldn't run or hide. He'd stand tall and look them straight in the eye. After all, he was in grade four now.

But there was no one on the stoop except a scrawny gray cat mewing hungrily from the second step.

"Oh my God! What happened to your face?" exclaimed Aunt Sophie, when he ran upstairs. "I bet those hoodlums you hang around with dragged you into a fight. You see what happens when you play with rough boys? Does it hurt? Should I get you a cold compress?"

"No. It's fine now," said Joe. "And ..."

"Good," said Aunt Sophie. "What a day I have had. Some young hoodlum stole all the money in my purse just as I was about to pay for my chicken. Why would someone steal from a poor woman? Now I have no chicken for soup tomorrow."

As Aunt Sophie continued to curse the thief who took her money, Joe thought about Sam. That thief could have been Sam or Al. That thief could have been

Joe himself, if he'd gone along with their plans.

"Aunt Sophie," he said, interrupting her moans about the thief. "They moved me up to grade four today at school."

In an instant, the pained look on Aunt Sophie's broad face disappeared like a dark cloud after a rain. "I always said you were smart as a scholar," she said, hugging Joe tight. "It was just a matter of time till you spoke English like an American."

"And I'm going to look for work tomorrow. I'll find a job and help out with the rent and food," said Joe.

Aunt Sophie's eyes filled with tears. "You're a good boy, Joseph. A blessing to your poor aunt after such a terrible day," she said softly. "You and Anna are like my children. You are like the children my poor Herschel and I never had. How proud Herschel would have been of you today. That boy is a real American, he would have said."

There was such warmth and pride in Aunt Sophie's voice that Joe knew that despite Aunt Sophie's complaints and worries, she was happy to have them with her.

"Maybe no chicken tomorrow," said Aunt Sophie, ruffling Joe's hair, "but thank God, there's a little strudel left for a celebration. How about a piece with some tea?"

"Thanks," said Joe, suddenly ravenous.

As Joe hungrily bit into the strudel, he felt a surge of hope about school, about New York, about everything. Then he remembered Anna and the letter. Had she mailed it already? Was it already on its way to Russia telling their parents not to come to America?

If only he could convince her to give New York another chance. Even cities deserved another chance. Maybe New York wasn't paved with gold, but it had Central Park, the subway, beautiful bridges and no threatening

Cossacks hiding in the woods. Best of all, New York was full of new chances, new possibilities.

"Anna! Anna!" he called as soon as she walked through the door later that evening. Then he blurted out all the things that had happened to him at school that day.

"Well," said Anna smiling. "That's wonderful."

"And I'm going to find a job and help pay for food and rent. You'll see Anna, things will get better for us in New York."

To Joe's surprise, instead of an argument, Anna gave him a hug. "Maybe you're right," she said. "After last night, I too have hope."

"Last night?" said Joseph, astounded at the sudden confidence in Anna's voice and face.

"I went to a meeting with Rose Finkel," she explained, kicking off her shoes. "The room was filled with people just like me who work day and night for low wages in miserable conditions. There were girls at that meeting who spoke in Yiddish in front of the whole crowd. And would you believe it, people listened to those girls. I learned that people are striking to get paid more, work less and be treated with more respect. I am so happy that I am not alone any more."

"Then you're not writing Mama and Papa to stay in Russia?" Joe blurted out.

Anna stared sternly at Joseph. "Did you read my letter?" she asked.

"Well, I saw it on your bed when I went for Aunt Sophie's shawl. I couldn't help it. I know I shouldn't have but ... "

"That letter is gone," said Anna.

"You mailed it?" asked Joe.

"No, I ripped it up," said Anna, laughing suddenly. "I was feeling so good when I came home from the meeting, I changed my mind about sending it. You see, I didn't just listen to speeches last night. I spoke up at that meeting."

Joe stared at Anna in disbelief. His shy, timid sister spoke up in a room full of strangers?

"My knees shook like laundry on a line," said Anna, "but I stood up and told everyone in that hall in Yiddish about Lucy and conditions in my factory. I told them how the bosses treat us. I told them that with such low pay and terrible conditions, we are left with little hope for our future. And hope is what we need. Otherwise, what is it all worth?"

"And they listened?" asked Joe.

"To every word," said Anna.

Anna's face glowed as she spoke. Joe had not seen her this happy since they arrived in New York.

"So how about teaching me some English now, Joe?" she asked.

"Joe? You're calling me Joe?"

"Why not?" said Anna. "Joe or Joseph, you're still my brother. Of course, I don't know how Mama and Papa will feel about your new name. Perhaps we should wait and tell them in person when they come to New York. What do you think?" said Anna smiling.

"Yes! Let's wait," said Joe, returning her smile. "And when they come to New York, we'll show them all the wonderful places there are to visit and by then, you will speak English like an American, Anna. And I'll get a job and soon we'll all be together. Imagine Anna! Mama, Papa, Aunt Sophie, you and me. We'll be a family in America."

Born in Germany, Frieda Wishinsky was raised and educated in New York City. Her thorough knowledge of the city shows in *Just Call Me Joe*. She knows what it feels like to be an immigrant kid and she loves how New York has taken in people from so many places, how they've become part of a vibrant ever-changing landscape.

She is the author of many other books, including *Each One Special* (Orca, 1998), which was nominated for a Governor General's Award, and *So Long Stinky Queen* (Fitzhenry). Frieda lives in Toronto with her husband, her 16-year-old daughter and her 22-year-old son.